Cally & Friends

Purrfectly yours,
Cally

As told to her Staff,
Sally Humphries

Graphic design by
Payne & Ink Creations

Cally and Friends is dedicated to
Richard and Celia Elzay of Crewe, Virginia.

Their love and care for even the most hopeless of four-footed creatures is an inspiration to all who know them.

Prologue

I'm back! With new friends, new adventures, and new wisdom. After all, I am older and wiser – theoretically.

Nonetheless, I am still the fun-loving ball of fur that you came to know and love in *Cally Tales*. And my Widow is still my staff. I have much to tell you about my friends, old and new.

The change is that I now live in rural Virginia without a basement or mice, although there are exotic spiders and stink bugs to hunt. Then, too, I have come to terms with d-o-g-s. I can't say the word yet, and I wouldn't go so far as to say all d-o-g-s, but some.

Read on and never hesitate to send fan mail. I love to be appreciated.

On a sad note, I lost my beloved cousin and dear friend, Precious, the Senior Cat Advisor to the World at Large. Memorial tributes are appreciated – but not in catnip. Greenies were Precious' favorite treat. I will partake in her honor.

 5

OLD FRIENDS

The Great Escape

I hate restrictions. Every closed door is a challenge – especially the one that keeps me indoors when I want to be out. My big incentive to be out the door is Mystery Cat, the debonair white cat with black patches that roams the neighborhood. Mystery Cat has a swagger, a fascinating twitch of the ears, a veiled look – all of which intrigue me. Whatever could he be saying with his slow blinks? All I can do in return is wiggle my ears and pretend to be shy. How all that comes across through a closed window is anybody's guess. I live in a buttoned-up air-conditioned house that affords no screened doors for flirtatious conversation.

The first time my Widow left the door open, I leaped for freedom. I made a quick dive under a nearby car but forgot to tuck my tail. She panicked and grabbed my tail, the only appendage available to her, and pulled me out from under. I was deeply humiliated, but not repentant. Next time, I said to myself, I'll remember to tuck.

The next time came, and I tucked. This time she was powerless, and by the time she collected her wits, I was out from under the car and exploring the backyard. It was a night-time escape, and since my night vision is a hundred percent better than hers, I could see her, but she couldn't see me.

I sniffed my way through the grass and shrubs, but Mystery Cat was nowhere to be found. Where could he be? Only this afternoon he had given me meaningful slow blinks, as if to say, "I'll be here waiting whenever you can get out." I felt foolish and filled with dark thoughts. Maybe I wasn't the only indoor cat he did slow blinks with. Maybe he had a neighborhood route, like the postman. Maybe he had a harem.

9

I headed over to the fence to give it one last sniff when my frantic Widow came prowling by with a bright light and a bag of my favorite treats, calling "kitty, kitty, kitty" -- as if she had forgotten my name. We met behind the trash barrels, and I was scooped up and returned to the house. I was too depressed to fight back.

Exile

*T*he opening of the outside door is now carefully managed to prevent my escape. The game plan is to coax me into the bedroom with Greenies, my favorite treat. There I remain, a prisoner in my own house, while visitors, workmen, or family members come and go. I use my prison time wisely -- either to solve the problems of the world or to wonder why I was stood up.

Besides using exile as discipline, my Widow resorts to mind-numbing logic. "Cally," she says, "do you really know what's lurking in the backyard? Do you think the security light goes on at night for no reason?" Before I can answer, she tells me. "Of course not. It goes on because there is some animal prowling about. Some beast of the bush who is hungry for cat thigh."

She might have a point, but I have options. In this high-tech age I can network my social skills on Facebook and pick up friends all across the country.

Oliver

*O*liver, my friend who lives two houses down in my former neighborhood, is still an item of interest. Oliver is adventurous as well as handsome. He sneaks outside whenever possible. He is not going out to explore the neighborhood, as I would, but to stake out a place in the grass and pretend he is a lion in the Serengeti. What an imagination! Sometimes it takes a yell or clap from his Daddy human to bring him back to reality. At other times, he is so lost in his Serengeti that he has to be picked up and carried back to the house and told to resume his duties.

And Then There's Max

*M*ax, my other New Hampshire friend, has been out of touch for much too long. I have new information about the little pockets at the bottom of cat ears, and I think it is important that he know. He told me those pockets were his glove compartments where he kept valuables, and he said it in a very matter-of-fact way. Of course I believed him because he was older and wiser and seemed to know things.

But now that I think about it, he may not be older – because no one knows where or when he was born. Urban legend has it he liked living in garages, so he roamed about until he found a garage he liked, then claimed it for his own. That's how he came to live in my New Hampshire neighborhood.

Even when the garage changed owners, Max stayed on, considering himself to be part of the property transfer. He continued to show up at the back door of the main house and wait to be fed. If the food was not acceptable, he went next door to see if he could do better.

Eventually Max was outfoxed. The family who fed him moved to a new location – and took Max with them. Oliver thought Max was taken by force, due to the paw-like skid marks in the driveway. Others in the neighborhood thought he was bribed with food. Whichever it was, he disappeared, and I miss him.

He was a true friend. He rescued me from the daily torments of the uppity chipmunks who paraded by my front door and teased me about my not being able to go and come as they could. In fact, Max laid out the leader of the bunch at the bottom of my front step. When I say "laid out" I mean Max "did him in." I owe him big time.

That's why I need to get word to Max about those little pockets at the bottom of his ears. He may think they are glove compartments for his valuables, but my sources say they are also hiding places for ticks who are looking to dig into meaty flesh ... either his or some unsuspecting human. At the very least, Max might be an unknowing tick accomplice.

I know ticks. They are schemers. It's not difficult to imagine one tick asking another, "Shall we walk the neighborhood, or ride the cat?"

Bones, Deena, and Boo

*T*hese good friends started life together in Alabama, then moved north to be near the grandchildren of their humans. I met Boo on Facebook, and she introduced me to Deena and Bones. Deena, the motherly one, does most of the talking. She is delighted that they have moved from a condo to a home near a lake with a basement and stairs. The stairs were frightening for all of them at first because no one knew what stairs were. But now that they do, they love racing up and down.

As for the basement and the possibility of mice, Boo has never seen a mouse, much less caught one. Bones and Deena, however, did some lizard captures in Alabama before Boo joined them. I haven't heard them talk about the taste of lizard – only about the number of corpses they left under the living room furniture. I'm more interested in the taste.

It seems that Bones also spent time on the street where she may have caught birds for a living. Even now she shows signs of the killer instinct when a bird flies by her window. It's only a guess but it could be early memories kicking in.

Closets and Warm Places

*T*he main attraction for Deena, Boo, and Bones in their new home is closets. All have sliding doors which are easy to pry open. Inside are warm sweaters. Boo, who has a particular fondness for warm things, is now bedding down among the sweaters for her afternoon snooze. Of course, that annoys her humans because of the cat hair she leaves behind.

I think the solution is a no-brainer. Listen up, humans. Dedicate some closet space to cat blankets (a fancy name for inexpensive throws) and call it a day. As long as the cat blankets are warm, who cares that they are not sweaters?

As for me, I do not have closets with sweaters. They are all in dresser drawers, and my Widow rarely leaves these drawers open. Some of you may be fortunate enough to live with humans who never bother to close dresser drawers. Enjoy! But be watchful for the domestic quarrel that escalates into drawer slamming. A drawer slammed shut can be breathtaking -- literally.

I prefer to hunker down in the linen closet, not only for warmth, but for meditation. Towels are as good as sweaters in my opinion. The builder of my new house took a narrow deep space, put shelves in it and called it a closet. It's dark and very private. Family members see only my eyes when they come looking for me, and only when I decide to open them.

Precious Is Still On My Mind

My cousin, Precious, the Senior Cat Advisor to The World At Large, taught me many things – the first of which was how to get an early breakfast. Her Mama human was not an early riser, so when Precious was tired of waiting, she leaped about the bedroom, hither and yon. Then she found a book and sent it crashing to the floor. Sometimes two books. Sometimes an alarm clock. Whatever was handy.

I do not have books in my bedroom to work with, but I have adapted. I do the head sit. I pounce on the bed with a thud, announcing my presence. Then I climb onto my Widow's pillow and sit in her hair, purring full blast. Usually she gets the message and pads into the kitchen in her bunny slippers (the ones with the rolling eyes) to dish up my breakfast.

The other morning, however, extreme measures were needed, so I tipped over her bedside glass of water. She was on her feet in a flash, and although I had to exercise patience until the wet spot on the carpet was cleaned up, my dish was filled and my day could begin. I told myself I was doing it in memory of Precious, who has now passed over to wherever cats pass over to. I miss you, Precious. Rest assured, I'll never forget what you taught me.

Gracie and Jakey

Gracie and Jakey, the black and white kittens from the Orphanage, finally adjusted to the new baby that suddenly appeared at their house. They had assumed he came from the same place they were from and was returnable. Precious told them they were delusional. She further said in no uncertain terms to "get over it" and "get on with it because life is short." And reading their minds, she advised life would get shorter if they laid a paw on him. Precious had a way of narrowing her eyes to slits when she laid down the law. The kittens backed off and got on with it.

Then came Baby #2, and Jakey took Gracie aside and said, "Let's give it up, Gracie. At this rate, we'll soon be outnumbered." Magnanimously, they decided both babies could stay.

Truth be known, Gracie and Jakey are mellowing. They cuddle together in the recliner like an old married couple. That doesn't mean they don't wrestle and romp at the end of the day. It's only that they are less feisty than they used to be, although Gracie remains a spitfire and still hisses.

Pippin and Elsa on the West Coast

I met Pippin on Facebook when he lived in North Carolina. He was a mighty hunter who once bagged a rabbit and hoisted it into the house through his cat door. Pippin never revealed how he did this. He only smiled the classic cat smile when asked – which means he wasn't telling -- ever.

Pippin also operated a "search and rescue" for Elsa, a Siamese of sorts, who was his housemate and got hopelessly lost whenever she went outdoors. Elsa lacked a sense of direction and always depended on Pippin to round her up and bring her home. It was a good working arrangement until the day she wandered into the street and was hit by a car. Fortunately, a neighbor came to Elsa's rescue and took her to a Vet. When her Mama human caught up with the news, Elsa was still trying to focus her eyes. She had a concussion, but she was otherwise intact.

Shortly after that, the family moved to the West Coast and a high-rise condo. There were no more cat doors and no more outdoor adventures. Pippin and Elsa are being rehabilitated as "inside cats." Pippin is said to be plotting an escape, but he hasn't managed to pull it off yet.

I Think I'm Cured

I think I mentioned my two attempts to bolt and explore the great outdoors. Both were short-lived and unfruitful. Forgetting to tuck my tail betrayed me in my first attempt, and the Mystery Cat stood me up in my second attempt and made me feel like chopped liver.

Then came my third escape. I was meandering around the storeroom one morning looking for a sunny spot to snooze when I smelled fresh air and began investigating. The door was open a crack. I threw my weight against it, and it opened! The great outdoors was suddenly mine. I leaped about like a rabbit in a carrot patch – exploring and sniffing until I had my fill and was ready to go back inside for lunch and a nap. Where was that open door?

The wind had closed it – tight -- there was no way back inside. Surely my Widow will come looking for me. Then I noticed. No cars in the driveway. The family was not at home. Yikes! How long would they be gone? Suddenly being on my own in the great outdoors was not so great.

As I wandered about, I saw something strange near the backyard shed. It looked like bones and a hunk of fur. Could it be the remains of the Mystery Cat? Come to think of it, he hadn't come calling in a long while. I remembered how the security light went on at night, and how my Widow asked if I thought that happened for no reason. She suggested it might mean there were strange animals on the prowl, hungry for cat thigh. Double yikes!

Hours passed and nothing changed. I told myself they would be home soon and find me missing. My stomach said it was long past lunch time. I nibbled some grass. Ugh. It wasn't very filling. I thought of napping, but under the circumstances a nap might make me easy prey for one of those strange animals that tripped the security light. Best to keep busy and vigilant. Time passed – very slowly.

I finally heard cars in the driveway, then my name being called. I scooted over to the storeroom door where I could be easily spotted. My Widow usually looked in the storeroom for me when she couldn't find me anywhere else. Our eyes met. I ran for the front door and a grand reunion. I think I am cured of my urge to bolt. I have been in the great outdoors, and it's not so great.

NEW FRIENDS

Now it is time to introduce my new cat friends...

The Incomparable Suki

I met Suki on Facebook and was completely atwitter with the color of his eyes. They are a mysterious shade of green that is absolutely fascinating. I thought that he must have come from a faraway kingdom on the other side of the sea -- perhaps the Emerald Isle. But no, it turned out he came from Cat Rescue, and, like me, he was only six weeks old and barely weaned when he was adopted.

The difference was that his family chose him from an online glamour photo, while my Widow was persuaded to take me because I had been dumped on a busy street and left to die. Then, too, Suki snored while I sigh.

Suki always seemed older and wiser somehow. He knew things. One day he gleefully said he had been on a walkabout in his backyard. How did he manage that? I wondered. He was an indoor cat, like me. How did he escape? I was desperate to know.

He ignored my probing questions and went on and on about the wonders of falling leaves and the twittering of the birds. The truth finally came out. His teenage human had talked him into putting on a harness and being walked about on a leash like a d-o-g.

I was stunned. Surely not. He admitted he wasn't crazy about the harness at first, but then he decided he didn't hate it. Besides, it was a beautiful green, the color of his eyes. Masculine ego, I said to myself. Is there no limit?

The "H" Word ...

Cat harness is something I remember from my kitten days when my Widow tried to put me into one. Someone had given her a jazzy harness and assured her it was possible to walk me around the block like the neighbors did their d-o-g-s. This was not in the Cat Manual, and I had no intention of doing such a thing. Nevertheless, with the help of a friend, she managed to strap me in. I tore around the house, trailing the harness up and down the stairs, and almost had a heart attack before sinking into the carpet, exhausted and humiliated beyond words. My body language was very clear. My Widow heaved a sorrowful sigh and released me. We never mentioned the "H" word again.

My New Outdoor Friends

*A*s chance would have it, I discovered three new friends who live in the outdoors and consider it beneath their dignity to be indoors. Their home base is an open deck, attached to a screened porch -- a safe haven which keeps them out of storms and away from hungry black bears. But they don't necessarily take all their meals at home. It seems they sometimes get bored with the same old food and go to neighborhood houses to beg.

Shasta is a Siamese with beautiful blue eyes, and the other two, Calvin and Hobbes, are handsome hunks who have lived in the neighborhood long enough to think they own it. As a trio of hunters, they turn squirrels and chipmunks into dead meat whenever they set their mind to it. Maybe I need a screened porch -- or a deck -- or a new diet.

My Diet is Boring

No chipmunk, no squirrel, no mouse. Nothing but turkey, turkey, turkey or fish, fish, fish. It comes via UPS in a case of twelve cans, and it keeps coming and coming and coming. I notice my Widow doesn't eat the same food for every meal. Why should I?

She says cats in the wild eat the same basic protein every day, so not to fuss. Problem is, I don't live in the wild. I am an indoor cat, and I deserve special treatment for the curtailment of my native instincts. I plan to go on strike for variety. While I'm at it, I think I'll lay down the law about cat litter.

Litter Should NOT Be Made Out of Corn

My Widow listened to another cat-loving human rave on and on about something called The World's Best Cat Litter and was completely taken in. She ordered a twenty-eight-pound bag. Twenty-eight POUNDS! How long will that take to use up?

To add insult to injury, this World's Best stuff has a funny color. It's made of corn and is a disgusting yellow. I prefer traditional grey. I immediately sniffed my disapproval. I walked back and forth in protest. I rearranged the litter. I crossed my legs. I considered using the carpet in the living room. She pleaded with me to reconsider. Emotions ran high on both sides, but I finally gave in and answered nature's call, thinking dark thoughts about the color. I may get used to this new litter, or I may not.

Mr. Kat's Litter Box

*I*n the mountains of North Carolina lived Mr. Kat, who won the hearts of the folks who adopted him when he needed adopting. He was an indoor-outdoor cat and quickly took to hanging out with his humans when they did their gardening. One day he took particular interest in a shrub they were trying to get in the ground. It seemed to take them forever to dig the hole, but he was patient.

When the hole was finished, Mr. Kat jumped into it and matter-of-factly proceeded to do his business. When finished, he jumped out with a look of gratitude and a nod that it was okay to cover it up. He could hardly believe his good fortune. His humans had gifted him with an outside litter box without his having to lift a paw.

Such consideration led him to expect the same when snow covered the ground. He could have cleared away the white stuff himself, but he discovered that his Daddy human did it faster with something called a shovel. He lobbied for shovel help and usually got it.

Back to My Litter Box Dilemma

I have decided The World's Best Cat Litter can stay. It's still yellow because of the corn, but it is serviceable. That is to say, it serves my purpose. Besides, I can do really good sand dune sculptures with it. This is an important consideration because I am sometimes bored and need things to do.

I must also tell a litter box secret. My Widow isn't as spry as she used to be, so she puts my litter box on a small table to do the required scooping and refreshing. She thinks this cuts down on the bending and stooping. That makes sense. However, one time she got distracted and forgot to put my box back on the floor. What to do? After considering my options, I decided to be the silent martyr. I hopped up on the table and did what I needed to do without saying a word. The next time she came into the area and saw the litter box perched on the table, she felt so mortified she brought me a double treat and her deepest apologies. Sometimes it pays not to make a fuss.

The Story of Paz

*I*magine being trapped in a storm drain. That's where my friend, Paz, found herself when she was five weeks old. She couldn't see the hand that reached down to rescue her because her eyelids were crusted over. She had pneumonia and was only days away from exiting the planet, but she survived with the help of two sympathetic humans and their Vet.

Life moved right along until her sixth year when she sprouted a lump on her nose. When she heard her Vet say the word tumor, she was puzzled. When he zapped the lump and made it disappear, she cheered. Then in a few months the lump came back. Now what? She heard the word surgery, but she had no idea what it meant, so she let it happen.

She wondered why her humans kept watching her nose. And watching her nose. And watching her nose. When several years passed, they stopped watching her nose and she heard the word cure. Now they brag about her in glowing terms. They say, "She is the only kitty we have ever known to have a nose job."

Paz Ages Well

*N*ose job behind her, Paz is now a senior citizen at age fourteen and stays active playing her favorite sport -- ice hockey. She uses an ice cube for her puck, and bats it all over the house, confident she is a great athlete.

Paz is also a talker and has her own jargon – a chirpy sort of meow that delivers her precise thoughts. Like most talkers, she follows her humans from room to room, seeking a conversational opportunity. The kitchen is ideal for cornering them because they can't escape as easily as they can in the living room. Besides, when food is being prepared or eaten, everyone is ready to talk.

In the morning Paz gets up at the crack of dawn to help her Daddy human do his computer work -- which means she walks the keyboard and blocks the screen. When that proves too exhausting, she slides into his "in basket" and purrs happy songs.

If the weather is cold, she parks her furry little bottom on one of the floor registers or hangs out in front of the wood stove with Ashley, her feline companion. Her front paws are usually crossed -- but nobody knows exactly what that means.

Ashley, the Companion

*A*shley lives in the same house and helps Paz keep in shape with a friendly chase around the kitchen and beyond. Even though Ashley eats like a horse, she maintains her youthful figure with a daily routine of chasing The Magic Red Laser Ball or The Wand Adorned with Feathers. The morning begins with The Red Ball and morphs into The Wand.

She is not above dragging The Wand around the house looking for someone to play with her -- or to find it when her housemates put it out of sight. She knows exactly where they keep the stash of new ones and will not be denied. Ashley is equally as determined about lap-sitting. She stalks laps like a bloodhound and hasn't seen a lap she doesn't want to nap in.

What school of higher education taught her these things? Not a single one -- unless you count the local lumber yard, where Ashley began life under a wooden pallet. Her humans wanted a male kitten to ride herd on their female house cats, and when Ashley came on the scene, they thought they had found him. Ashley jumped into the arms of the Daddy human and closed the deal before he found out her gender. Smart girl.

Tripper

After Ashley came the adoption of Tripper. A befuddled neighbor heard meowing in the wheel housing of his truck and sighted a ball of fur inside. The challenge was how to get her out. Nothing seemed to work until Ashley's human put food in a Havahart cage, sat it beside the truck and let hunger work its magic. Out came a bewildered kitten. Since the neighbor figured he must have driven forty miles with this fur ball rolling around in the wheel housing, it was logical to name her Tripper. She still looks a bit bewildered but is otherwise a beautiful Calico.

Tess

I have heard about feral cats, and I think I almost was one. I was a pound and a half and barely weaned when I was dumped on a busy city street and told to take care of myself. If I had followed that advice and set up a life for myself on the streets without human contact, I would have been labeled a feral cat. I would have avoided humans like the plague and acted wild when approached. Lucky for me that a lovely lady spotted me diving into the wet weeds and never gave up until she had coaxed me out of my hiding place. She even found a home for me.

Tess was not so lucky. She wandered about, seeking food, and ended up joining a colony of other destitute cats who gathered at the back of a gas station, scrambling for scraps

of food. A cat-friendly human started feeding the colony regularly, and Tess scampered out, tail held high, to welcome the meal-giver with a cascade of meows. Highly unusual behavior for a feral.

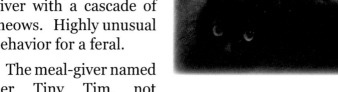

The meal-giver named her Tiny Tim, not knowing her gender. His wife, however, recognized a fellow female, even if she was a scrawny grey tabby kitten. Tiny Tim became Tess, in memory of Dick Tracy's comic book girlfriend Tess Trueheart. Tess agreed to leave her feral friends at the gas station for life on the farm with humans. Today she is a lovely, plump gentle kitty who is still the first at the door to greet her human staff with a welcoming meow.

In return, she wants a belly rub on her pretty, soft, doughy underside.

Zoe

Zoe was also a feral cat, but so tiny that she was knocked out of the way by the bigger cats when the meal-giver came with food. She seemed destined for starvation until the human spotted her dilemma and decided to try a rescue. She was taken home to his farm and given barn space with Tess and Tripper for an adjustment period. Large screens allowed all three to see what was going on outside but not to make an escape.

Zoe, the scrappy one, felt hemmed in and starting climbing the screen, looking for an exit. Somehow her hind foot caught in the wires, and she was soon hanging upside down. Thankfully her cry for help was loud and pitiful. X-rays at the Vet showed a crushed foot, so she had to be persuaded to drag around an orange leg cast and to wear a big blue collar to keep her from chewing off the cast. Lesson learned. She calmed down and became a cute, fluffy kitty who had a poem written to commemorate her ordeal. The poem is still on display at the Vet's office.

Reckless

***R**eckless*, a beautiful long-haired grey, is a friend of a friend, and she definitely has a mind of her own. Back in her kitten days, her human dreamed of mating her with a long-haired white to produce a litter of splendid grey and white long-haired kittens.

When Reckless went into her first "mother mode," a blind date was arranged. Trouble was, no one explained the grand plan to Reckless – or if she had caught the drift, she wasn't buying. Like a prim and proper Victorian, she sat firmly on her haunches and seemingly muttered under her breath, "No way, Buster."

Back home, her human decided to keep her inside and let the heat of the moment pass before making a trip to the Vet. Reckless responded with long, loud, dragged out cries of anguish. She not only had hormones to deal with, but now the stress of not being able to go outdoors when the mood struck her. She solved both problems in short order by clawing the screen door to shreds and disappearing over the hill without a backward glance.

Two days later she was escorted home by a scruffy, black cat with scratches on his face and half an ear missing. He gentlemanly left her at the shredded back door and said his goodbyes, never to be seen again. Reckless was filthy and flea-infested and her long hair was matted and muddy – but otherwise she was intact and happy. No one was surprised when four black kittens came forth from her adventure. Only one survived.

The Cat and the Gas Stove

*T*his story is truly hard to believe, but it comes from a tax assessor, and they usually don't kid around. It seems the Assessor Lady came home one day and found all the gas burners on her kitchen stove blazing away. Somehow her cat figured out how to turn on the knobs. She's sure it was the cat, and Tax Assessors are not careless with their facts. Who taught him that? I wonder. I don't even know his name.

Chapeau

I never met Chapeau because he was fiercely independent, coming and going as he pleased, sometimes for days at a time. Maybe he was doing his version of the Australian walkabout. Then one morning after a long absence, his human saw a lifeless black and white blob in the street. The fur was familiar but not much else. Poor Chapeau, she thought, he was on his way home but forgot to check both ways. She determined to give him a respectable funeral.

It was a hot summer day in Virginia and the red clay soil was as unforgiving as cement. With grit, fortitude, and a pickax, Chapeau's human and her daughter fashioned a respectable grave. Gently they lowered their beloved pet into it, bowed their heads, and uttered tender words of remembrance. Tears flowed freely as they shoveled the soil back in place.

An indignant meow was heard close by. It was Chapeau, home and hungry, wondering what all the tears were about. Didn't they know he always came back? How could they mistake him for a clumsy beginner who didn't have enough sense to duck and dodge cars in the street? He began immediately to milk his miraculous return for all it was worth.

Sandy, Stormy, and Smokey

*L*ike me, Sandy and Stormy are Calicos, who were the last of the litter and eager to be adopted into a home where they could run the show. Smokey, however, was in a center and marked for "Kill," until a husband and wife team stepped up and took the three as a package. Their names were inspired by the musical group Earth, Wind, and Fire thus they became Sandy, Stormy, and Smokey, the Triple S's. That was six years ago, and the once-upon-a-time orphans now rule an otherwise childless household.

The trio begin their day early – with a four o'clock breakfast. Since their humans have an ever earlier start time, there's no grumbling about the meows before daybreak. The fun begins once the humans are out of the way. Running through the house like cannon balls, free-for-alls, snacking when hungry and snoozing in their man-made trees is the normal routine. They have six cat trees at their disposal, two of which are on a screened porch.

The porch is a mixed blessing. The Triple S's can smell the fresh air and see the birds, insects, lizards, and hummingbirds – but they can't lay a paw on them. Their humans think it's a hoot to watch them try. Do they care? Not one bit. They would much rather be laughed at then forced to endure creep-and-peep traffic, grumpy bosses, and water cooler gossip. A cat's life has unique perks.

Ming, Max and Maddy

*M*ing was a beautiful Lilac Point Siamese who was adopted by a retired Navy Captain needing   company when he became a Widower. Ming was young and eager to produce beautiful kittens but when her Widower took her to the breeder to begin the process, Ming refused to cooperate. She had scruples. No one-night stands for her. She wanted a long-term relationship.

Thinking it best not to argue with a Siamese, the breeder introduced her to a young Blue Tonkinese named Max. With the blessings of all, Max and Ming began a relationship that produced three litters of gorgeous kittens. When asked about their long-term marital harmony, Max said it was no mystery. He learned from the start to always agree with whatever Ming had in mind.

Ming, however, was not blessed with long life. Max grieved quietly at first and then lobbied to move in with one of his daughters. Still being his agreeable self, he let his daughter have the last word; and the rumors began to grow that Max was henpecked. Maybe so, but he outlived his strong-willed daughter and found a new soul mate in a Blue Point Siamese via the internet. Maddy, or Madalyn Rose, was an experienced mother thirty times over, and was ready for a peaceful retirement. Max and Maddy get along famously, I am told. Max, the perfect gentleman, keeps his thoughts to himself and as always, lets his companion run the show.

Cadence's Almost Fatal Curiosity

Cadence is one of Ming and Max's daughters whose curiosity almost killed her. First it was the "thumb-ball" mouse in the center of the computer keyboard which she attacked and demolished along with the four surrounding keys. She pretended to be the wide-eyed innocent. Didn't they say it was a mouse? Didn't they expect her to eliminate the mice in the house? Her staff made the necessary repairs and forgave her, deciding it was an honest mistake. They kept the computer closed thereafter.

Cadence returned to the scene of her crime a few months later to discover some mending and a threaded needle. Being curious about the taste of this strange new thing, she swallowed the needle whole and bolted from the room with the thread hanging out of her mouth. When her human caught up with her, even the thread had disappeared.

The Vet took X-rays and found the needle and thread in her stomach and advised that surgery was possible but that the conventional wisdom was "sharps will pass." Keep a watchful eye on Cadence and on her litter box, was the Vet's advice. Three days passed and Cadence showed no signs of distress. Her litter box, however, produced a waste deposit the size of a tootsie roll with the needle in the center and the thread connecting several segments. I'm not making this up. Not even a talented and imaginative Calico like me could think up such a story. I submit it's a tribute to an amazing Creator who designed our systems to protect us -- from ourselves.

Katie

Katie is one of my California friends who was born to be a blessing cat. To me that means she showed up wherever she found a human in need. In Katie's case the human was a Widower who didn't think he liked cats. Not a problem. Katie only smiled her mysterious cat smile, and went into sales mode. Never pushy, always agreeable to being fed whatever and whenever the Widower thought best, she slowly won his heart and made him smile. Soon Katie was invited to ride shotgun with him when he toured the property in his golf cart. They became best buddies.

When the day came for the Widower to quit this world for the next, Katie stayed by his side until his lifeless body was discovered. Then she waited patiently for her next assignment while the property went up for sale. The Widower's daughter was so touched that she drove forty miles every day to feed Katie and keep her company, all the time trying to persuade her own cat to make room for the youngster. No sale. Perhaps the new property owner would let her stay on? Again, no sale. I am truly befuddled. Who can resist such a lovely white kitten with a heart of gold? I plan to go into my secret place and think of someone.

Racer

Racer is another of my California friends. I saw her picture online and was immediately taken by her dark sleekness and bewitching green eyes. I could envision her having a glamorous career as a fashion model for a pricey cat magazine or maybe as a lap cat for one of Hollywood's jetsetters. Her name, Racer, might mean she raced from one country to another aboard her human's private plane.

Imagine my shock when I learned Racer lived in a home much like mine and slept most of her day on ordinary beds, floors, and furniture – like most of us. She even has to share things with a newcomer to the household, a terrier puppy named Rocky who chases her around the house as if it were his. Negotiations are underway for who owns what and for what part of the day. As for her name Racer – it came from a little girl human who loved her as a kitten and said she went "from zero to sixty in a split second. Let's call her Racer!"

The One and Only Trucker

*T*rucker lived down the street from Racer, but he was originally from Montana. He got his name, Trucker, because he was transported to California in a truck. I can't imagine traveling all that distance in a truck! Most of my friends can hardly make it to the Vet in a luxury sedan. But Trucker loved adventure. He probably begged to ride on the hood where he could feel the wind ruffling his fur and could give advice to bugs zeroing in on the windshield. That's pure speculation on my part. We never talked about his early kittenhood, partly because we didn't meet until he was a senior citizen; and by that time, he would have forgotten the bugs and the wind.

Trucker loved being part of whatever was going on. He was a friend to the friendless – a cuddler who enjoyed being held close to the heart. On the other hand, he never hesitated to speak his mind and let you know what he wanted, what he could not live without, and what you could do if you ignored his deepest desires. He was an independent thinker.

For a brief time, he assumed the title of Senior Cat Advisor to The World At Large when Precious gave it up, but his twenty-year-old body suddenly gave out, cutting short his reign. He left a trail of wonderful memories. Here's to Trucker, the Magnificent! And here's to his human who is now an emptynester! Perhaps she would like to take in Katie who is looking for a human to bless. I'm not above being a matchmaker.

D-O-G FRIENDS

*E*ven though I thought I would never befriend a d-o-g, I'm mellowing. It started when my Widow came home from her hairdresser six weeks in a row with d-o-g smell on her lap. My first reaction was horror. How could she betray me like that? Then I began wondering, what would Trucker do? He was an independent thinker and a friend to all. I hear him saying, "Consider the fact we are all four-footed with hairy coats as well as ears and tails that convey our thoughts. Face it, Cally, we're kindred spirits."

In honor of Trucker, I reconsidered. Remember, however, when you read their stories that dogs have masters while cats have staff.

Bella and Buffy

*B*ella and Buffy are Shih-Tzus and probably distant cousins of mine, since they are adorable and called lion dogs. I think I have a lion profile -- around the mouth, at least. I outweigh

Buffy, the smaller one, so I would not be overpowered if we met face-to-face. Shih-Tzus were originally bred as companion dogs for Chinese Emperors. They also served as foot warmers at night. I understand Bella and Buffy offer the same service today for their two teenagers. They choose a teenager and pile on her bed until they decide, by some mysterious means of their own, to switch to the other teen. How do they decide that? I wonder.

Potty Breaks and Baths

*A*n even greater mystery is that they sleep as long as their humans do and don't take potty breaks in the middle of the night. Considering that teenagers sometimes sleep until noon, this is a truly amazing exercise in bladder control. Even cats take midnight potty breaks on occasion, but because of our instinctive litter box training, we do the necessary things without dragging our humans outdoors in their pajamas.

I'm also smug about the self-sufficiency of cats in the bath department. I wash myself from stem to stern every day, using only my prickly tongue. Bella and Buffy require frequent soap and water bathing. They also need regular haircuts and ear-hair clippings. As for my maintenance routine, I admit to coughing up hairballs which demand human cleanup – but only seasonally.

Belly and Buffy are smug about not shedding. I'd rather not talk about that because I'm a big-time shedder. Some humans avoid me like the plague because of my shedding – and my dander. Today everyone seems to be allergic to something. But are cats the only culprits? I think not. Frankly, being accused of all the allergies in the world makes me feel like a second-class citizen. This could lead to depression if left unchecked.

Exercise/Playtime

*M*ost of my cat friends will admit that dogs get more exercise than cats. Dogs walk their humans around the block and stop here and there to lift a leg and fertilize something. Sounds intriguing. Bella and Buffy carry exercise to a higher level with the indoor coffee table chase. Heads down, tails up, on your mark, GO! Round and round the coffee table. Then, by some mysterious signal they stop and reverse direction. This switcheroo goes until one or both have had enough. I admit it does wonders for their physiques. Neither of them has a sagging tummy like mine.

The best I can do without an exercise partner is the classic tail chase. My routine is to pretend not to look at my tail, while looking at it over my shoulder. When the time is right, I pounce on it and seem to mean business. Sometimes I give it a bit of a nip as though it belonged to someone else. Sometimes I hiss at it like a villain -- in case someone is watching. Always I end up letting the poor thing loose, so that I can begin again.

I do the tail chase wherever and whenever the mood strikes me. If there are guests in the house, I use the corner of the shower stall for privacy. I am determined to keep doing my tail-chasing exercise for many reasons -- one of which it that my extended staff is beginning to call me "Fats." I need to put an end to that. It's not good for my self-esteem.

Murphy and Wally

Murphy is my Texas dog friend who appears frequently on Facebook. He's big enough to eat me in one bite, but I think he prefers dog food. An Australian Labradoodle, he's very friendly and can be persuaded to walk off with almost anyone who bats their eyes at him, but I hear it wasn't always that way.

As a puppy, he had a serious hip problem and was labeled a troublemaker who should be put down. A real grump, they said. Hmmm. I'm guessing he was confined to a cage too often for too long – which would make anybody grumpy. Not to mention the pain of trying to walk on a hip that didn't follow directions.

All of that changed for Murphy when he was adopted by a dog-loving couple who owned Wally, another Labradoodle who was as frisky as he was friendly. Wally coaxed Murphy into romping and playing, which was good hip therapy. Along with fish supplements, vitamins, a diet of raw beef and organ meat, Murphy's hip problem disappeared.

Now both dogs are in their senior years, playful as puppies and completely addicted to their ultimate treat -- cheddar cheese. They know when the refrigerator opens and the cheese drawer is pulled out. Not so for the lettuce and celery drawer. Labradoodles are as smart as cats – well, Murphy and Wally are.

Sugar

*S*ugar lives not too far away from me, although we have not formally met. I hear she's part Lab, Dachshund, and Cocker Spaniel but I don't know which part is what. She was a rescue, like me, but on a county road in below zero weather. Her mother and siblings died, leaving her forlorn and sad. She weighed only eight pounds and had hyperflexion and other ailments in her front feet. The Vet gave her flashy red stents for her legs, and her family named her Sugar because she was so sweet.

It took only three weeks for her legs to recover so she could be a frisky, playful puppy. She lives on a farm where there are moles and voles to hunt down and soybean fields to dig up. Her family forgives her for the digging because she is a superb watchdog – not to mention a walking buddy for the lady of the house.

Wilma

Wilma was born in Indiana, a mix of Schnauzer and something else. At least she had the face of a Schnauzer. She was part of a neighborhood litter that sent pint-sized boys and girls scurrying home to ask their mommas, "Can we have one? I'll take care of it!" How many mommas have fallen for that line? The clincher was that the momma dog was reputed to be a non-shedder.

That's how Wilma found a home and a chance to prove herself. Legend has it, although I wasn't around to verify the story, that she grew into a bewitching damsel who was also a creative thinker. For example, she loved peanuts but didn't like waiting around for someone to break open the shells. She learned how to do it herself, having a peanut feast whenever the opportunity arose and leaving the cleanup for others. Did she have peanut breath? If she did, no one complained. She also took her baths in the tub like Cleopatra -- as if they were beauty rituals and not a duty to be endured.

Her life changed drastically when her family moved into an apartment. No pets allowed. Wilma considered her options and started buttering up the grandparents, the ones who still had the big house and yard. She sat at their feet, docile as a lamb and always on the small rug provided. She came when called. She fetched. She entertained. She took everything in stride, even car rides over bumpy roads.

In return, the grandparents gave her filet mignon or took her to McDonalds and ordered her a cheeseburger from the kid's menu. Sometimes they shared a little of their ice cream.

The good life proved to be too good. Wilma developed

a heart problem and never recovered. Her memory is cherished today. She is at rest at the home of the lady who, as a little girl, promised to take care of her.

Freddy

*I*ce cream must have something going for it that has escaped my attention all these years. Freddy, a small blond terrier who was best friends with a soft-serve ice cream devotee, made so many trips to the local Dairy-Treat that he became a full-blown addict. Whenever he heard the words, "Would anyone like some ice cream?" he raced to the car, planted himself by the passenger's door, and waited. He didn't care if it was ten minutes or fifty, his mind was made up. Freddy would NOT miss a trip to the Dairy-Treat. Maybe he knows something I don't.

Rags

*R*ags was a white English Springer Spaniel with the heart of a hobo. A Virginia family offered him food and shelter when he wandered into their backyard, and he decided to stay. The urge to roam, however, never left him and it soon became clear that Rags needed to be hitched to something secure.

He had an exercise run between two trees in the backyard, but one day when he was seeking a new view of the world, he talked a family member into fastening him to a large iron lawn chair in the front yard. All went well until the mailman came strolling up the walk. If there was one human Raggs wanted to wage war on, it was the mailman. He may have had good reasons, but he never bothered to say what they were. He simply took off after the mailman at a full run, dragging the clunky lawn chair behind him. The mailman picked up speed, Raggs moved into high gear, and the lawn chair banged and bumped along, followed by a ten-year-old family member yelling at the top of her lungs for Raggs to stop.

The backside and legs of the mailman escaped harm. The lawn chair survived, and Raggs, having vented his feelings, put the whole thing out of his mind and allowed the mailman to continue his duties to the household without further incident. All I can say is, don't mess with Raggs.

Schnitzel

I guess I have to admit dogs outshine cats in the protective custody department. Cats make great lap-warmers and adorable comfort-givers, but we lack the aggressive bark and bite of dogs – and it has nothing to do with our size. Schnitzel was a miniature Dachshund, yet she set herself up as protector extraordinaire to a toddler – a newcomer to the family circle, not by any means an old family friend.

When a strange man came to Schnitzel's house, she sized him up and decided he was not on the approved list for selling, delivering, or chatting. As soon as the Stranger reached down to pick up the toddler and pat her bottom, Schnitzel bared her teeth and sank them into his boot. She was a Type A decision maker. She didn't like what she saw. Case closed. When the Stranger came again, he was greeted with a growl. Schnitzel was not one to reconsider.

PBJ

PBJ's story began at the side of the road. He was only a puppy -- rescued by a kind lady and her two daughters from certain death. The girls decided to call him Peanut Butter and Jelly, or PBJ for short. In turn, he decided to repay his rescuers by becoming Super Dog, Protector of Women -- his women. Whenever an unknown person or vehicle came into the yard, PBJ went into attack mode. Even though he weighed a mere ten pounds, he made enough racket to rattle dishes. It was impossible for his women not to know they were under attack. This was very reassuring for the ladies who had been left to manage for themselves -- the man of the house being always gone – or almost always.

Then one night quite late, the missing Dad reappeared after a long absence, without notifying his ladies, and without considering PBJ, Protector of Women. PBJ assumed the worst and bit him in the leg. This did not go well for PBJ. But who can blame him for doing what he thought best?

Woodie and Gus

Except for Ming and Max, most of my cat friends had their beginnings in orphanages or worse. Few were ever purchased from breeders. I don't think any of us had humans who travelled hundreds of miles to pick us up. Should we feel like second-class citizens because of our humble beginnings? I think not. However, it's nice to know how the other half lives.

Woodie and Gus are Labradors, advertised for adoption as puppies. They attracted the attention of a couple of Lab lovers who piled into their truck and went to the kennel to take their pick of the litter. The Labs came in two colors, black or brown. Since they couldn't decide which color they liked best, they took one of each. The brown was named Woodie, and the black, Gus. The challenge was fitting the very large "puppies" into the container brought for the trip home. So much dog, so little space.

Once home and settled in, Woodie became the protector of the lady of the house. He was always at her side, even killing spiders for her. Soon he assigned himself the task of walking her neighbor -- even though the neighbor thought she didn't much like dogs. Woody convinced her he was not a bad sort – certainly no one to be afraid of. When he saw her walking on the road, he dropped what he was doing and joined her. There was no calling him back until he had returned her to her house. Who could resist such unselfish devotion? She developed a love for him in return. It's hard to figure how dogs decide these things.

Daphne and Samantha

By the magic of a glamour photo on the internet, Daphne went from the miseries of a street urchin in Tennessee to the royal life of a princess in Massachusetts. Now she lays on plump pillows and eats only homemade dog food, claiming store-bought food makes her sick. I heard she broke into the dog snack cabinet the other day and ate a whole bag of treats. I must tell you that dog treats are large treats, not the penny-sized cat treats I get -- so a whole bag of dog treats is no small thing. If she keeps that up, she will soon be strapped to a treadmill for weigh reduction. I have heard that she wiggles when she walks, but that may be a hip disorder and not jiggling fat.

Meanwhile Samantha, the elder dog of the house, has decided to become her guidance counselor. Sam, as she is called, is nine years old and recently had a pacemaker implanted to keep her heart ticking as it should. She frequently advises Daphne to chill and cease going stir crazy when her humans leave her for even a short time. Daphne ignores Sam's advice and immediately goes into face-licking and heavy panting as soon as her masters return. Maybe she's having a flashback to her street days in Tennessee. Maybe she is lobbying for a ride in the car. Dogs have strange ideas sometimes.

Cato's Dog Friend

Cato was one determined South Carolina cat, the lone survivor of a litter of kittens dumped over the fence into a country field. The rules of the property owners were specific. All castaways were welcome if they agreed to eat what the dogs ate and if they didn't cause trouble. Cato was not fussy about his diet, but he wasn't overly fond of the larger-than-life dogs who ruled the yard and field.

Nevertheless, when he spied one of the dogs taking a snooze, he climbed on his back and convinced himself that the canine was a mattress. By the time they both woke up, they were friends.

The Deka and Kitty Legend

*H*ere's another dog and cat story passed down by my ancestors. The legend begins with a grey and white kitten who was a Christmas present to animal-loving teenagers. Being a newborn, she arrived without a name, and there was a sharp division of thought on the subject. Should she be called Fluffy or Puffy? Should she be Alice or maybe Esther? The Daddy human decided the issue. "Her name is Kitty," he announced after hearing arguments on both sides. "Case closed."

Kitty ultimately had an outdoor life which brought dead mice to the front steps, and then a pregnancy. She chose the underside of a mattress as her birthing room and meowed her Mama human from the living room to the bedroom to be with her. It took three meow trips to get the thick-headed Mama to stay put on the bed. When the birthing was over, Kitty reappeared to make the announcement. It was a litter of one, a male whom the family named Skeezik.

Skeezik was nothing like Kitty. A trouble maker from the start, he traveled the house with his tail in the air like a runaway shopping cart, seeking things to destroy. As his habits grew worse, he was given a new home in another town. No one mourned his absence. Not even Kitty.

Kitty lost her motherhood capacity soon after and settled into a mellow middle age -- until the day Deka came. Deka was a grey wolf, posing as a German Shepherd for the benefit of the town authorities. Deka ruled the yard, Kitty ruled the house. One day they met face-to-face on the front steps, and Kitty greeted him with an imperial HISS. Deka, who could have eaten her as an appetizer, flattened himself at her feet. Surely a victim of total shock.

Although the Daddy human claimed Deka was afraid of Kitty, the family thought Daddy was not thinking clearly on that subject.

Tigger

*T*he Vet said someone apparently tried to kill this half-grown cat, but only knocked him out and left him in the woods where a precocious pre-teen found him. "Look what followed me home," was the way the young boy phrased it. Yeah, right, thought his amused Dad who had watched the two come home by boat.

The family soon realized Tigger, or Tig for short, was a few bricks short of a load and didn't have the foggiest idea what being a cat meant. Claws were a mystery to him, and he had to be taught to climb trees. When his humans went for an evening stroll, he followed along like a puppy, stopping when they stopped and patiently waiting for neighborly conversation to end.

Ultimately Tig concluded he was an invincible super dog. To prove his point, he decided to stare down a full-grown German Shepherd. When the Shepherd sighted Tig posturing on the front lawn like a commanding general, he moved in for the attack. Tig slowly turned and gave the Shepherd such an evil eye that the canine skidded to a stop in the newly planted grass and hightailed it home. Tig resumed his military stance.

Watching this, the Boxer who lived next door started doing reconnaissance before venturing from his front stoop. Tig decided it would be fun to ambush the big guy. When the moment was right, he sprang on the Boxer's back and rode him bareback as in a rodeo. I know this because Tig's human caught it all on camera.

It was finally decided Tig needed more space – like on a farm. His new venue seemed to suit him well, but he couldn't resist creating drama at the family reunion. From his secret hiding place, Tig made note of the long tables and the large crowd. He waited until everyone was enjoying the feast, then with the speed of a cannon ball he hurled into space and snatched a chicken leg from the hands of an astonished human, ran the length of the table and disappeared behind the barn. Trust Tig to make a dramatic entrance – and escape.

One Final Thought

*N*ow that I have expanded my horizons to include dogs, I might consider goats and chickens. One of the humans in my Fan Club loves goats. She trained a pet goat named Ginger to walk on her hind legs, to roll over, to play dead, to shake "hands," and best of all, to count to three. I'm flabbergasted.

This human also said she had a goat named Maureen who became best buddies with a chicken named Red. It began one summer with Maureen allowing Red to ride on her back. By winter, their friendship had grown to the point where Maureen was the warmth-giver for Red. On very cold nights she stood over her feathered friend to make sure Red was comfortable. I never met a goat, so I don't know how their minds work, but that might be something to explore.

Cally's Special Thanks

*T*o all my four-footed friends, especially d-o-g-s, thank you so much for allowing me to put my spin on your stories. Although I tried hard to stick with the facts you gave me, I occasionally slipped and added a personal comment or two. Sometimes I couldn't help myself.

Your staff or masters – as the case may be – also deserve recognition for helping you remember things and for sending me your glamour photos.

Here they are in alphabetical order:
Andrea Baker
Susan Baker
Ken Barnes
Phyllis Brown
Fran Cecere
Harleen Dizer
Liz Dykstra
Richard Elzay
Eric Erny
Faith Fondry
Sandy Griffin
Dee Langford
Jane Lumsden
Gail Matthews
John Mouring
Shawn Royal
Nancy Schlesinger
Shannon Smith
Nancy Wienstroth
Judy Zummo

Made in the
USA
Columbia, SC